D0381151

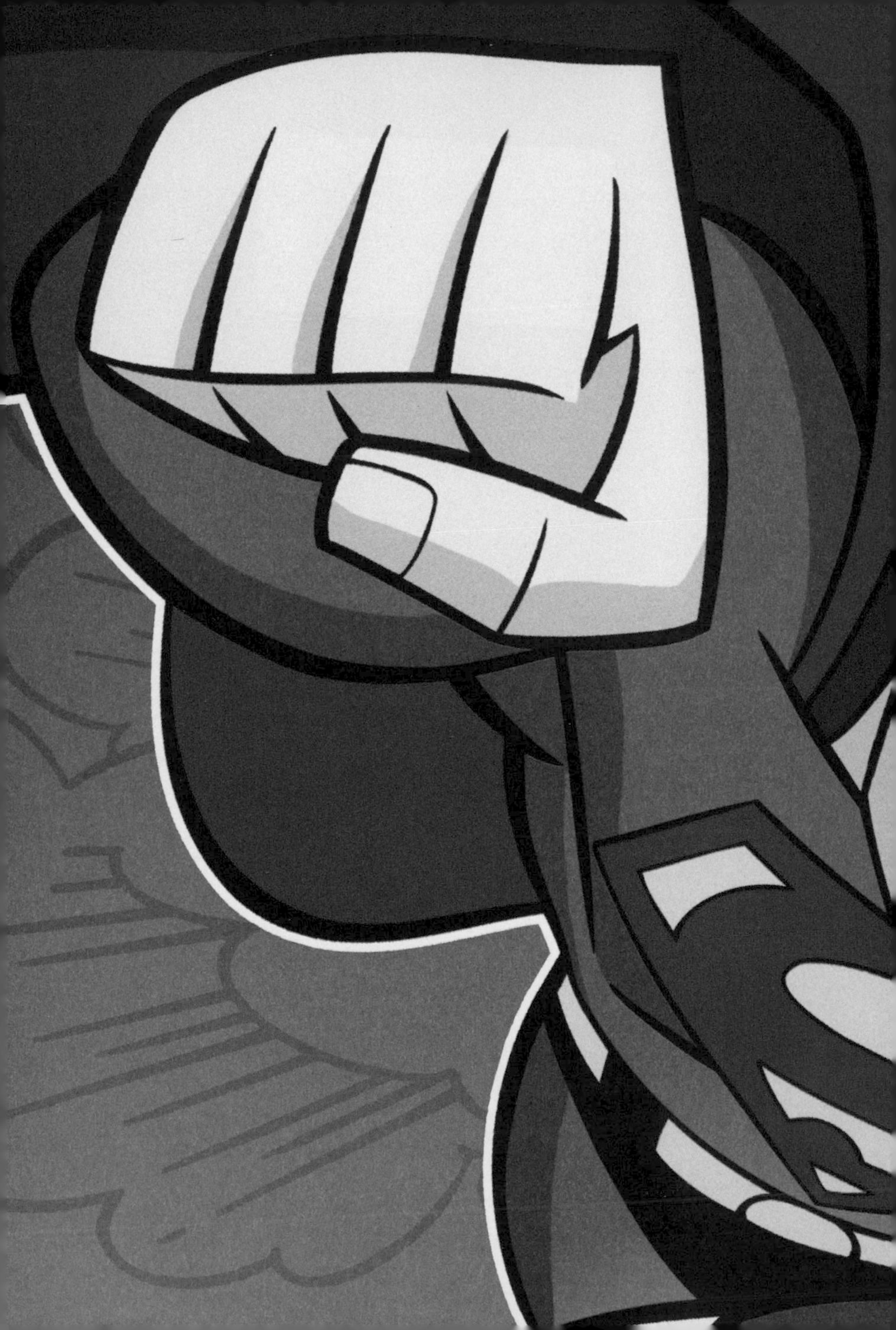

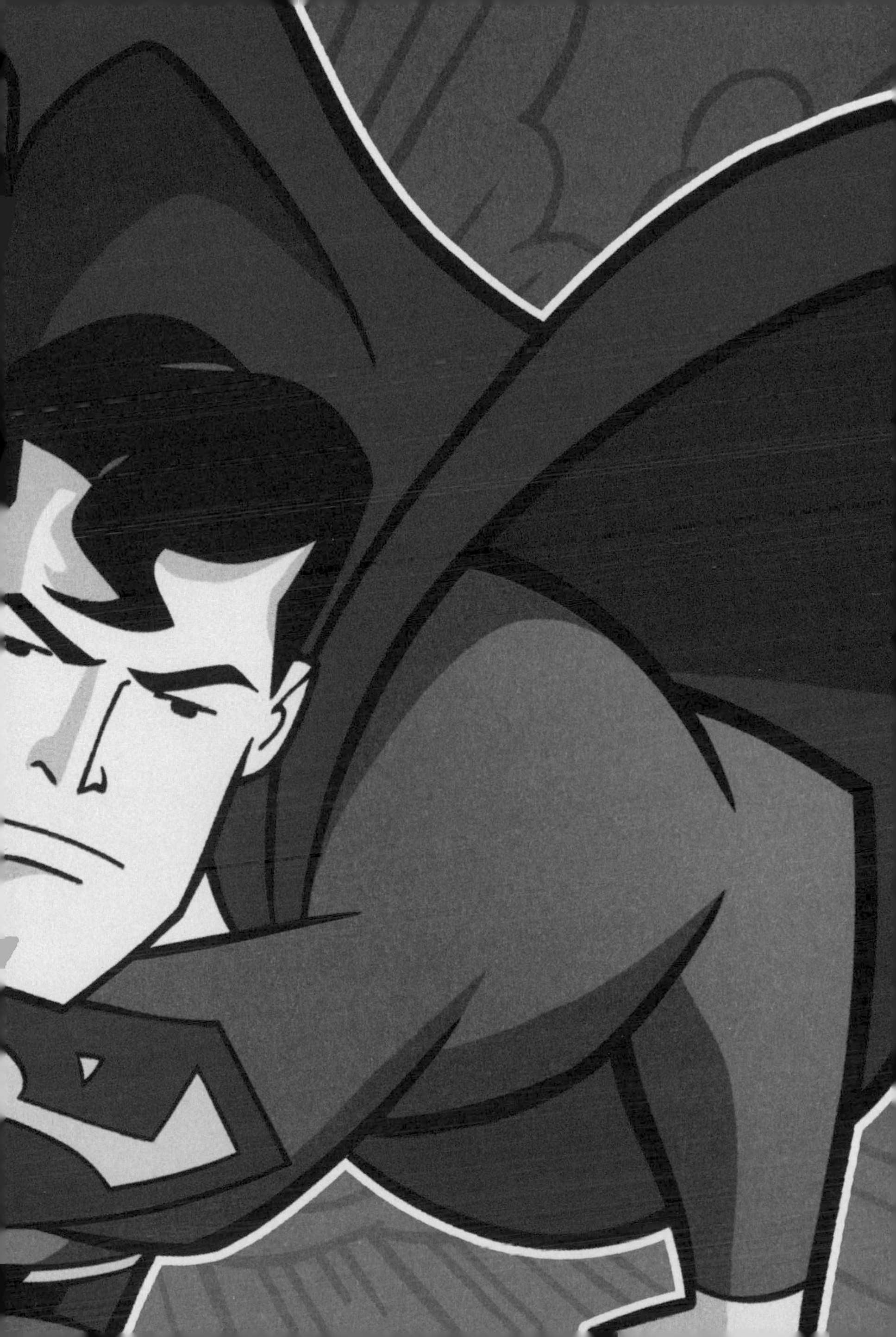

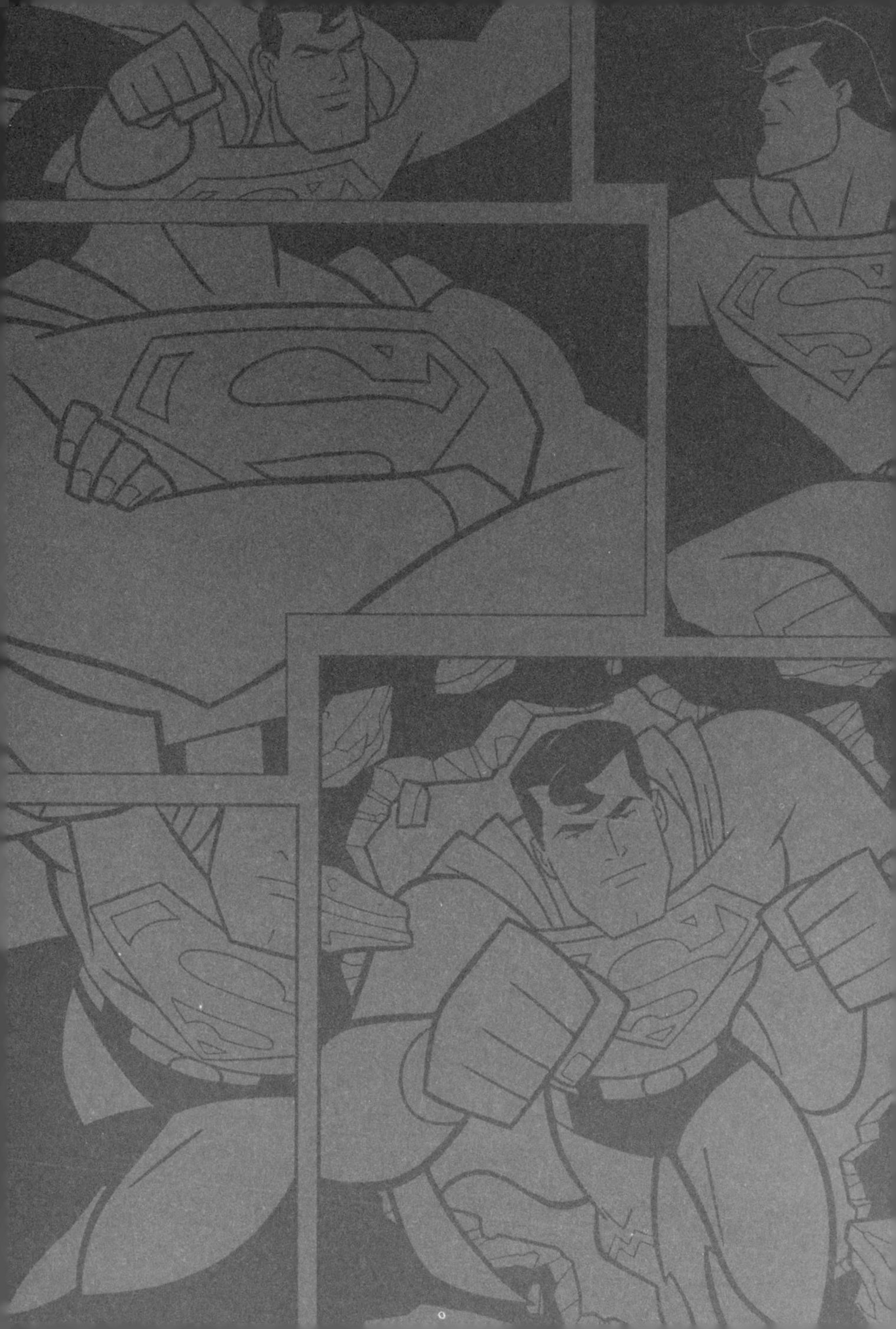

SUPER DC HEROES

SUPERMAN

THE STOLEN SUPERPOWERS

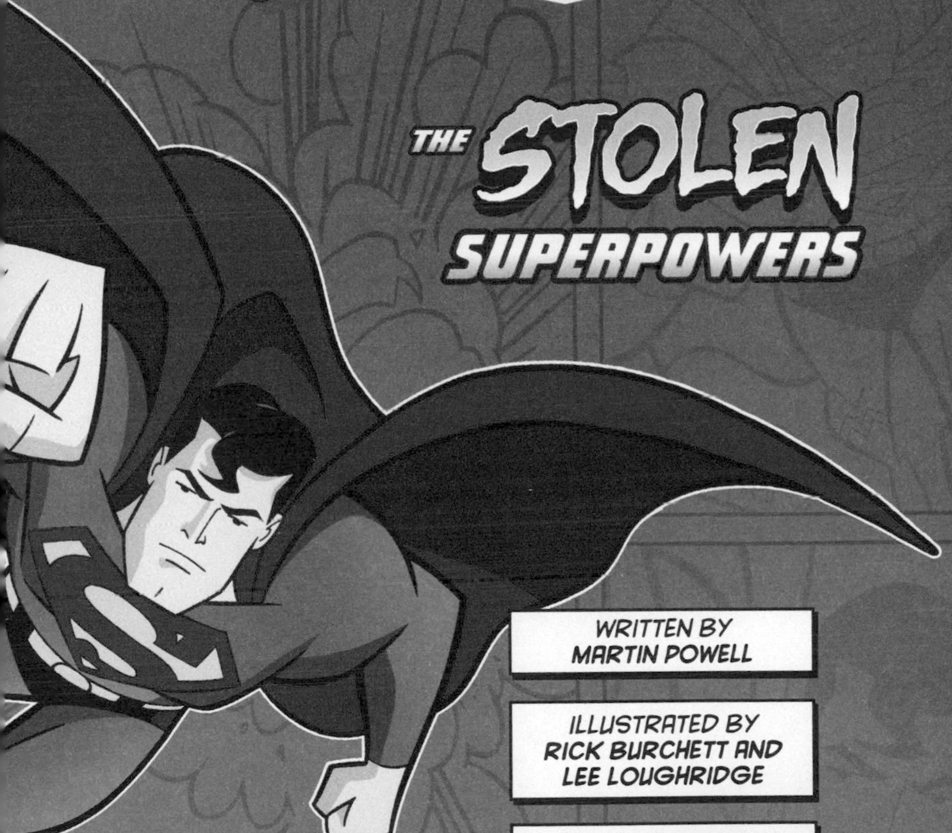

WRITTEN BY
MARTIN POWELL

ILLUSTRATED BY
RICK BURCHETT AND
LEE LOUGHRIDGE

SUPERMAN CREATED BY
JERRY SIEGEL AND
JOE SHUSTER

STONE ARCH BOOKS
MINNEAPOLIS SAN DIEGO

Published by Stone Arch Books in 2009
1710 Roe Crest Drive
North Mankato, Minnesota 56003
www.capstonepub.com

Library of Congress Cataloging-in-Publication Data
Powell, Martin.
    The Stolen Superpowers / by Martin Powell; illustrated by Rick
Burchett.
    p. cm. — (DC Super Heroes. Superman)
    ISBN 978-1-4342-1160-6 (library binding)
    ISBN 978-1-4342-1373-0 (pbk.)
    [1. Superheroes—Fiction.] I. Burchett, Rick, ill. II. Title.
PZ7.P87758Sto 2009
[Fic]—dc22   2008032476

Summary: Superman has his hands full. First, he encounters his cousin,
Supergirl, a reckless teenager with powers like his own. Then he confronts
a creature known as Parasite, who can absorb Superman's strength and
super-speed just by touching him. Superman knows enough to not shake
hands with the deadly fiend, but Supergirl is still learning the ropes. Filled
with her power, the Parasite now battles the Man of Steel in a fight that
rocks the planet. How can Superman defeat a villain who gets more
powerful with each punch?

Art Director: Bob Lentz
Designer: Bob Lentz

Printed in the United States of America in Stevens Point, Wisconsin.
112012
007036R

TABLE OF CONTENTS

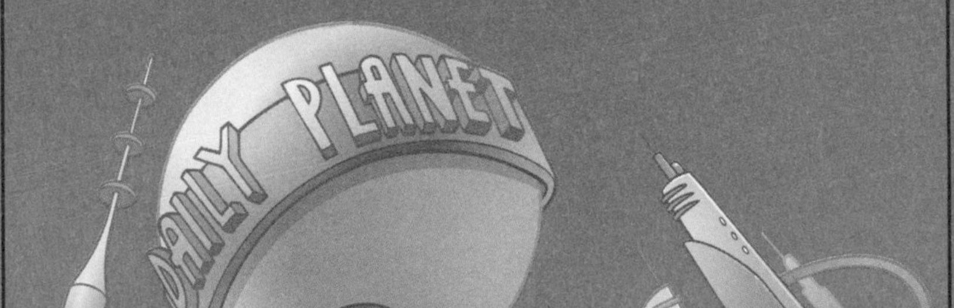
DAILY PLANET

CHAPTER 1

THE HUNGRY FLAMES

Swan Valley had never been a very exciting place. The small factory town, located an hour's drive from mighty Metropolis, was in the middle of a typical sleepy summer day. That is, until the fire broke out.

The lumber warehouse had started to blaze quite suddenly, spreading among the stored stacks of timber. In a matter of minutes, the entire place had become a crackling tinderbox. Melted windows billowed with blinding black smoke.

Sirens screamed in the distance. Nearly three minutes away, the fire trucks would be too late. The streets filled with frightened families and friends of workers still trapped inside the burning building. There seemed to be no escape.

Suddenly, there came a loud speeding "whoosh!" sound from the clouds. "Look! Up in the sky!" a store clerk pointed above.

"It's Superman!" an elderly woman whispered, in awe.

For a moment, many doubted their own eyes, although everyone knew that he was real. No one could ever get used to the spectacular sight of Superman in flight.

The Man of Steel's red boots landed on the pavement. Sheriff Stevens came running over.

"Thank goodness you're here, Superman!" the sheriff exclaimed. "Three men are trapped in there!"

"Not for long," said Superman. He sped immediately toward the burning building. His red and blue uniform blended into a colorful blur of motion.

The eyes of the crowd widened with disbelief as the hero passed unharmed into the roaring flames. The heat inside the warehouse was terrible. Poisonous smoke strangled the daylight into darkness. Superman was unaffected. He had, in fact, once walked upon the surface of the sun.

Through the thick smoke, Superman quickly scanned the warehouse. He sped from room to room, searching for the missing workers. As the flames grew, he feared all hope was lost.

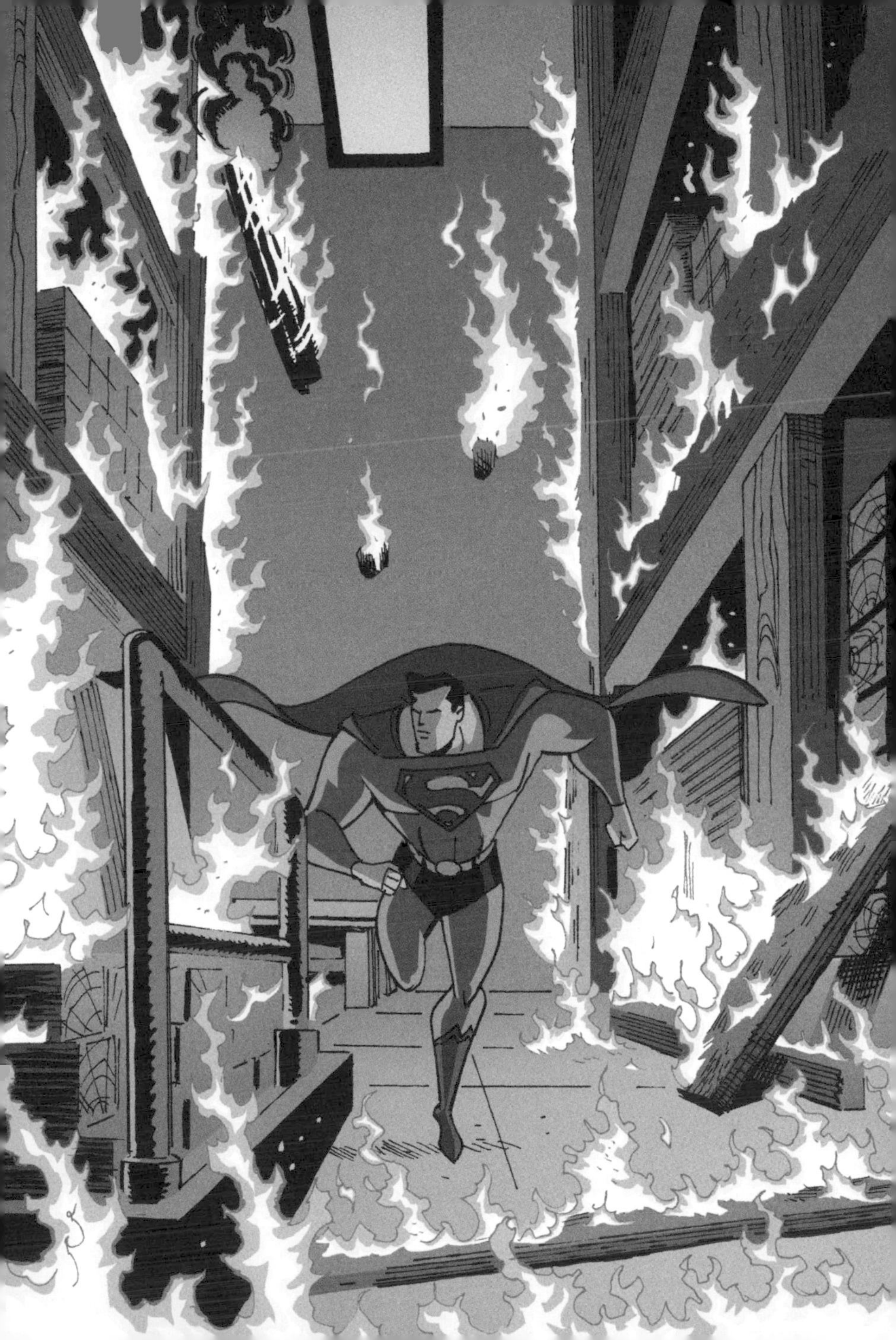

Then suddenly, Superman heard voices from behind a nearby wall. "Help! We're trapped in here," the voices shouted.

A large steel beam blocked the only doorway to the room. Superman knew he didn't have much time. He had to get inside before the angry flames got in first. Without hesitating, he lifted the giant beam into the air. He tossed it across the warehouse like a stick.

Superman swiftly kicked down the doorway. Smoke and flames poured into the room. When the men saw the famous scarlet "S" emblem approaching, they knew there was nothing left to fear.

"I'm taking you all out of here," said Superman. His deep, powerful voice boomed through the roaring flames. "Hold your breath for a few more seconds."

Unfastening his cape, Superman wrapped the warehouse workers safely inside. Cradling the men in a single arm, Superman soared upward, crashing through the roof. Before anyone could take a breath, each of them were standing safely outside the warehouse.

Everyone was out of danger, but the flames raged on. Fire engines raced toward the scene, but they were still more than a minute away. Superman knew he had to act fast or hundreds of jobs in Swan Valley would be lost.

Then, unexpectedly, a low sonic boom rang out. The remaining warehouse windows shattered from the sound. All eyes looked upward. A slender girlish shape of red, blue, and blonde streaked down from the sky.

Suspending herself in midair, the teenaged girl waved to the Man of Steel. Superman's blue eyes narrowed.

"Need some help, cousin?" the flying girl smiled. "This looks like a job for Supergirl!"

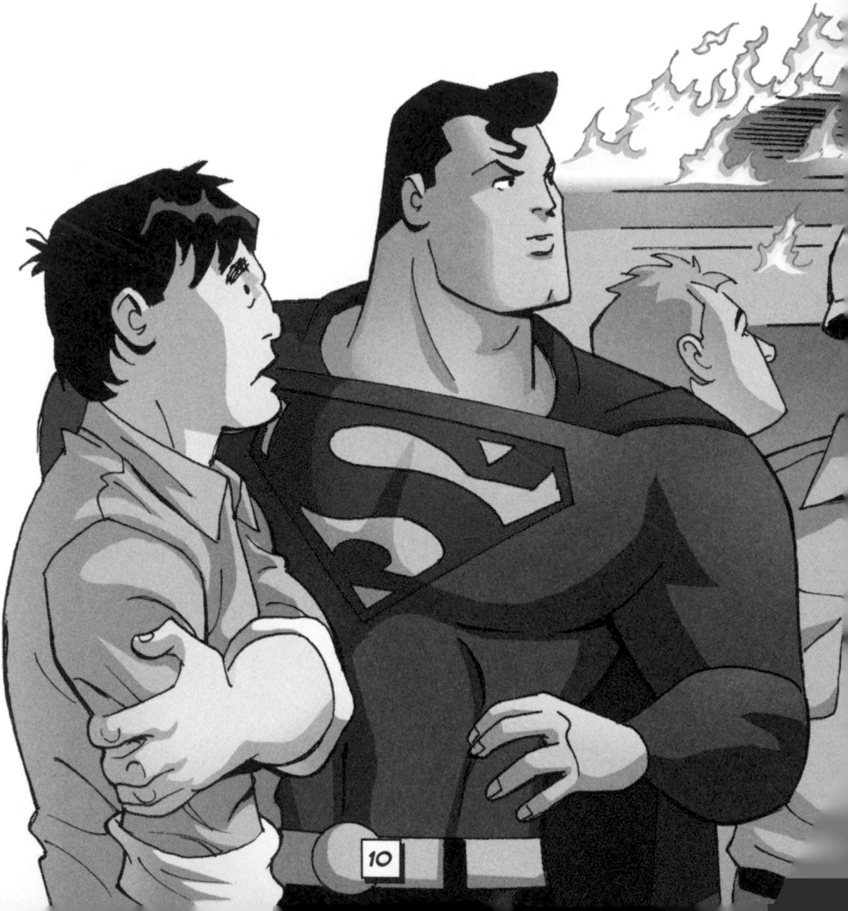

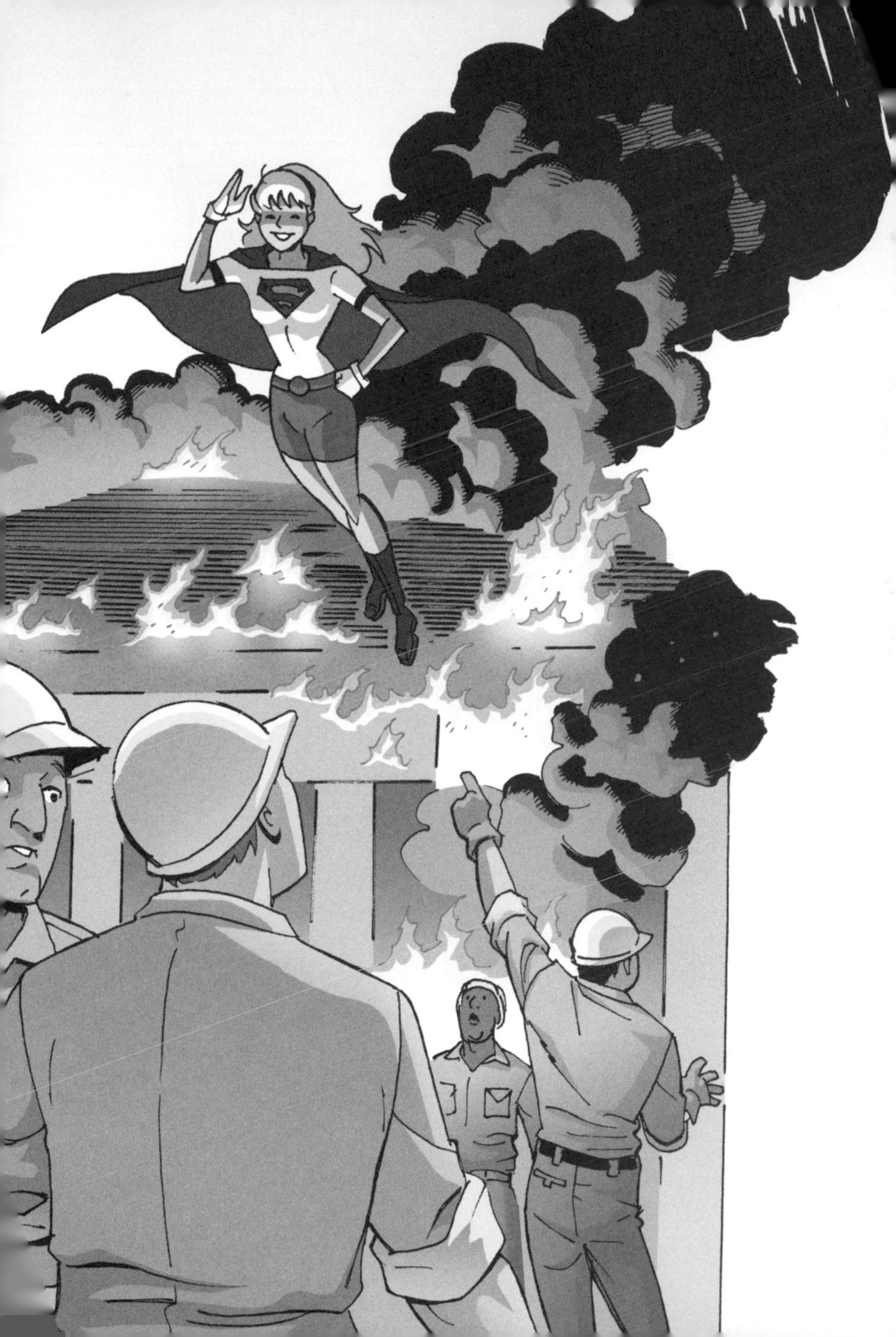

CHAPTER 2

THE GIRL OF STEEL

Supergirl's smile sparkled in the flicker of the growing flames. She sized up the problem with a single sweep of her super-vision. She was ready to save the day.

"This is a once-in-a-lifetime moment, folks. Get your cameras ready!" she said.

Superman sprang forward just as the teenager took a deep breath. "Supergirl! Wait!" he yelled. For once, even Superman wasn't fast enough. Before he could stop her, a deafening gust of wind blasted from the girl's lips.

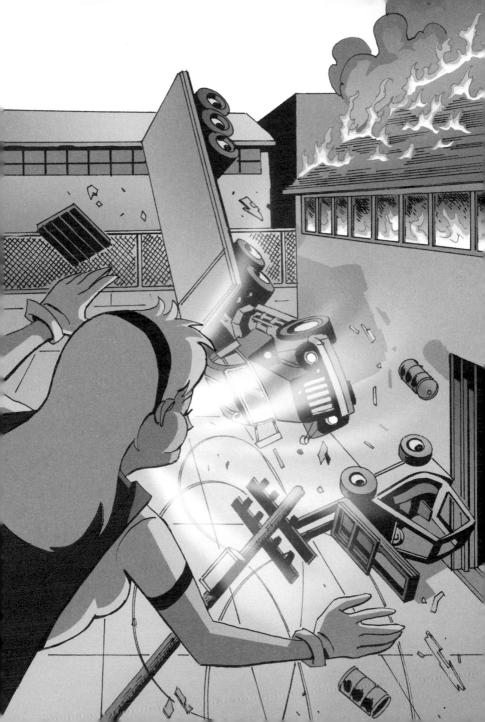

Telephone poles snapped under the gale. Steel streetlamps bent like rubber. At the first glance, the teenager's breath appeared to completely snuff out the warehouse fire.

Superman knew better. "Stop!" he said. He held Supergirl's arm. "You're spreading the flames!"

The girl gasped, realizing her mistake. Now the angry blaze had jumped over to the chemical factory next door. There were explosive materials stored within the burning walls — enough to blow half of the town off the map.

"I . . . I'm sorry, Superman. I didn't know," the girl's voice trembled.

"Keep the crowd back!" Superman ordered. He raced quickly toward the flaming factory.

A scan with his X-ray vision revealed that there was no one inside the building. *Good,* Superman thought. *Now to act fast.*

Superman gripped the side of the building, the pressure of his fingers cracking the thick concrete. He gritted his teeth. His superpowered muscles bunched and strained. With a mighty heave, the Man of Steel lifted the entire factory free of its foundation and over his head.

Then, Superman sprang upward. He flew into the sky carrying 200 tons of fiery concrete into the air.

After flying up more than a mile, Superman picked up speed, vanishing from view. He rocketed the giant inferno into the upper atmosphere. The blue sky faded, and suddenly the stars were plainly visible against the blackness of outer space.

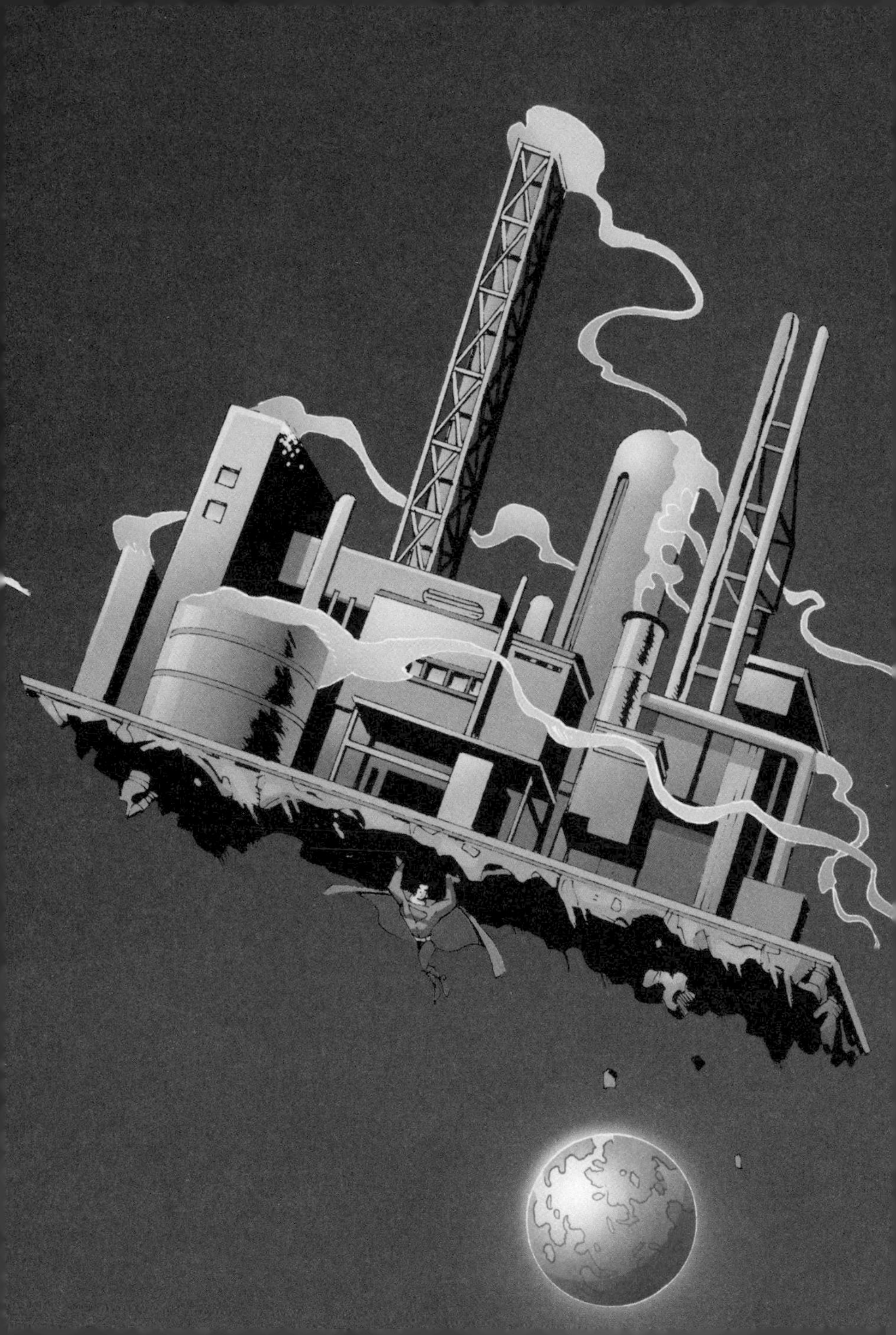

Superman soared higher and higher above the blue marble of Earth. In airless orbit, the flames of the factory quickly sputtered out. They smothered themselves from lack of oxygen.

As the temperature grew colder, the walls of the factory soon turned to ice. Even Superman knew he couldn't survive long in the harsh environment of space. Moments later, he returned to Earth. He gently settled the chemical factory back on its foundation.

"I know, I know. I blew it. Literally," said Supergirl. She was hardly able to look Superman in the eyes.

The crowds kept their distance. They were stunned by the miracles they all had witnessed. This would be talked about for decades to come.

"That was too reckless, Kara," Superman whispered. He didn't want anyone else to hear. "Someone might have been hurt."

"I only wanted to help," said Supergirl. She looked toward the ground, embarrassed by her mistake.

Superman gently clasped her shoulder. "You're still learning. Remember, lead with your brains, not with your powers," he said. "My super-hearing is picking up a bank alarm in downtown Metropolis. Help clean up this mess."

Supergirl's eyes lit up hopefully. "Bank robbers! Maybe they have laser rifles!" she said, clapping her hands excitedly. "If we fly to the city together we can —"

"You're staying here," Superman interrupted. "That's an order."

Superman took flight. He left the angry teenager standing on the Swan Valley street far below.

It wasn't fair, she thought. She could be a lot of help against bank robbers. No one would ever notice her if Superman kept her away from the action.

"Uh, excuse me, Supergirl?" someone called out from the crowd.

Supergirl glanced over her shoulder. She saw a man in a suit coming toward her.

"I'm the mayor of Swan Valley," he exclaimed, bowing. "Too bad that Superman has flown off. We want to have a parade in celebration of you saving our town. It's the very least we can do to show our appreciation. Since Superman isn't here, we thought you might be interested."

Supergirl wrinkled her nose, puzzling the question. She wasn't sure what to answer. What would Superman do? He probably wouldn't approve of such a public event. Still, he wouldn't stay mad at her forever.

"Sounds cool!" she said, smiling brightly.

CHAPTER 3

MONSTER ON THE LOOSE!

"You snooze, you lose, Clark," said Lois Lane. She grinned, waving the morning edition of the *Daily Planet* newspaper under the nose of fellow reporter Clark Kent.

"Congratulations, Lois," said Clark. "Two Superman stories in one day. What's your secret?"

Lois seated herself on the edge of Clark's desk, playfully swinging her heels. She always looked her prettiest while celebrating a new triumph. At least Clark secretly thought so.

"I might ask you the same," she said. "How'd you manage to scoop me on that factory fire?"

Lois pointed down at the newspaper. The morning headline nearly covered the entire front page: **SUPERMAN PUTS OUT FIRES.**

Clark fiddled with his tie. "No magic," he said. "Just a nose for news, I guess."

Lois frowned. Sometimes things just didn't add up with her quiet, mild-mannered colleague. She'd worked with Clark for a number of years, yet she still knew very little about him. Even so, all of her reporter's instincts told her that there was much more to Clark Kent than what he pretended to be.

"Lois! Kent!" yelled Perry White from his office door. "Get in here on the double!"

The two reporters leaped up from their chairs. Their editor-in-chief looked in no mood to be kept waiting.

White paced in front of his cluttered desk, his white shirtsleeves rolled up past his elbows. He gazed out the window for a moment at the gleaming towers of Metropolis. Fifty million stories were going on out there, and it was the duty of the *Daily Planet* to report them.

"Close the door," he said, barely glancing at Lois and Clark. "The mayor of Swan Valley is planning a parade this Saturday to honor Supergirl for saving their town. We still know so little about Supergirl, except that she's a survivor of the planet Krypton, like Superman. A Supergirl interview is long past due. I want both of you there to cover the story."

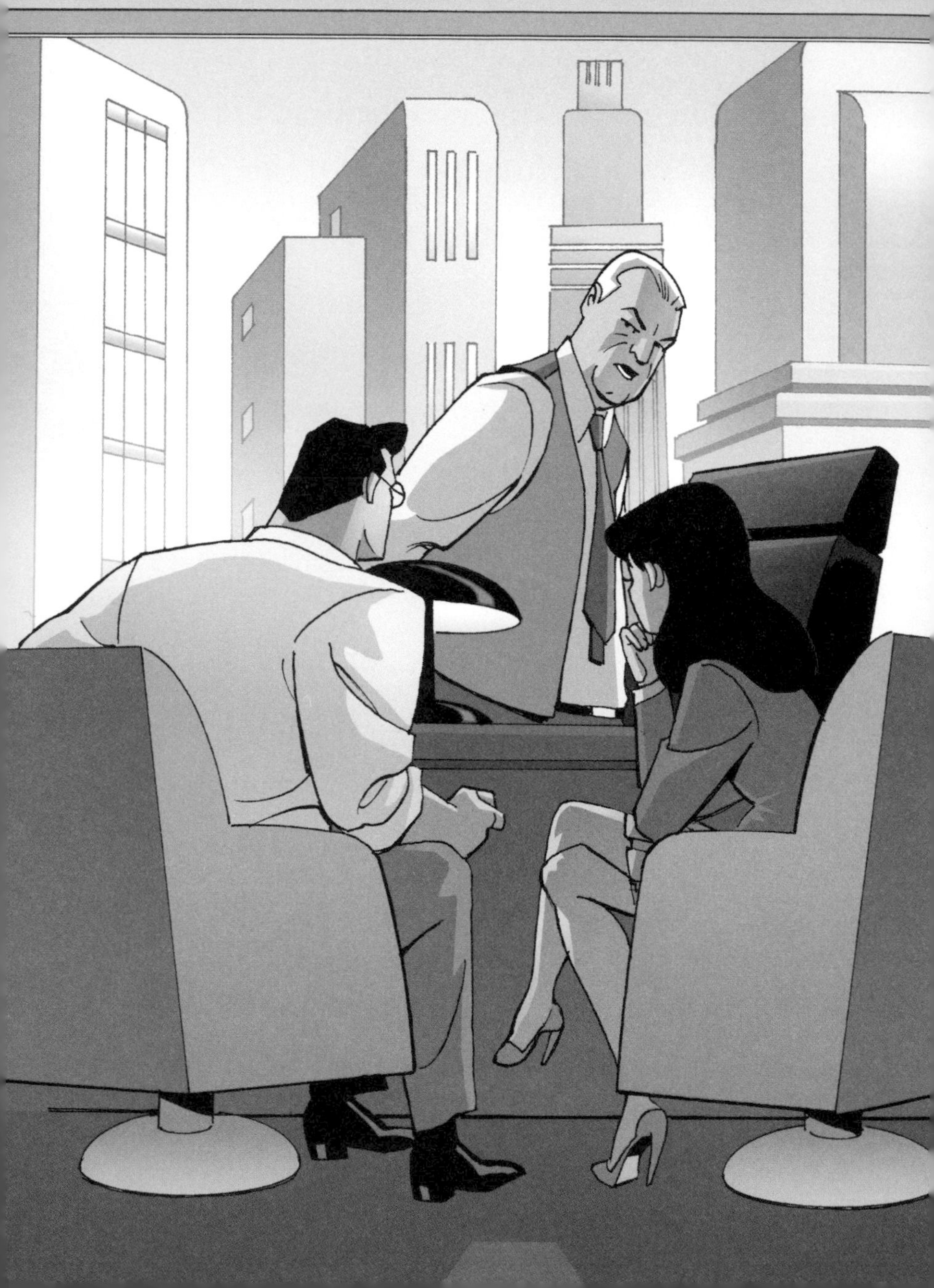

"Chief," Clark said. "My sources tell me that the Swan Valley fire caused a power failure at Stryker's Island Prison. The super-criminal Parasite is rumored to have escaped. I already have a couple leads to follow up and —"

White raised a rough-knuckled hand. "Nothing doing, Kent," he said, shaking his graying head. "I need you both at that parade. Lois can handle the interview. You'll talk to the locals for a home-spun feature article."

"But, the Parasite —" Clark began.

"Is much too dangerous for you to trail, Kent," White cut him off. "That monster can absorb all the strength and knowledge from anyone he touches. Anyway, he'd be a fool to come to Metropolis. You're going with Lois."

White turned toward the office windows. He stared back out at the glimmering Metropolis skyline. "Let Superman handle the Parasite, Clark," he said.

Lois hooked Clark's elbow with her arm and gave him a tug. For an instant, she was slightly startled at how steely he felt. "Come on, Clark," she said, pulling him out of the office. "I'm counting on you to help me blend in with the other hayseeds. It'll be fun, you'll see."

• • •

Night in Metropolis brought long shadows on the busy sidewalks. A tall man in a raincoat and hat snatched up a copy of the evening edition of the *Daily Planet* newspaper. He didn't bother paying the news vendor. His glowing eyes scanned the headlines.

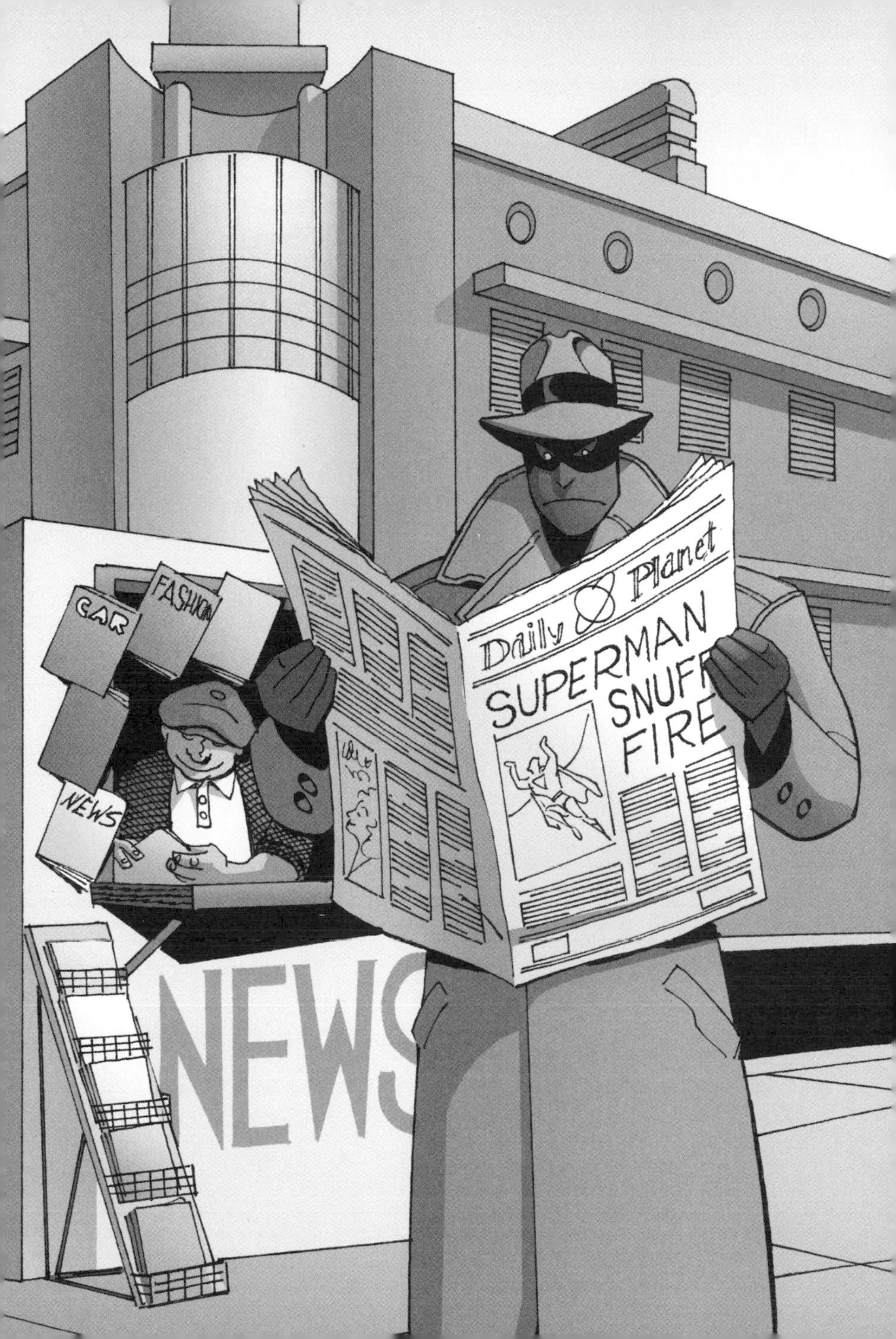
CAR
FASHION
NEWS
Daily Planet
SUPERMAN SNUFF FIRE
NEWS

"It's been a long time since I've seen a parade," Parasite said. Then he laughed beneath the shadows of his hat. "Be seeing you soon, Supergirl. I can hardly wait to shake your hand."

CHAPTER 4

TROUBLE ON PARADE

The Swan Valley streets were packed with people applauding the parade. They waved at passing floats, the town's brass band, local beauty queens, and colorful clowns. Every few minutes, all eyes peered toward the summer sky. Supergirl had not yet arrived.

"I hope Supergirl shows up," said Lois. "Or else this parade is going to be really boring. You don't suppose something bad happened to her, do you?" she asked.

Clark Kent shook his head and grinned. "Same old Lois," said Clark. "You can see something dangerous even in a small town parade."

"It's my nose for news, Clark," said Lois. "I can always tell when something bad is going to happen. Trust me. Something is wrong."

Clark Kent wasn't smiling anymore. He was busy watching a man in a raincoat and hat. There was something strange about him.

The man bent down to pet a dog on a leash. As soon as he touched the dog's fur, the man looked up. His ears, now as keen as a dog's, heard a faraway sound.

It was Supergirl flying toward the town.

Then the man bumped into a cart full of ice-cream cones. The man in the raincoat turned as cold as ice.

"Brrr," said a young woman standing nearby. "I'm freezing."

"Me, too," said her friend. "But the sun is still shining. What's going on?"

Clark watched the man in the raincoat and his strange behavior. As Clark stared, his X-ray vision allowed him to see beneath the raincoat. The man's skin was purple. It glowed with energy.

This is bad, thought Clark. *Very bad.*

Lois interrupted Clark's thoughts as she jabbed his ribs with her elbow, "Oh, look! It's Supergirl!"

The teenage dynamo soared downward, speeding out of the sky like a comet. For an instant, the entire parade hushed. Then, a roar of applause filled the air. Supergirl basked in the glory.

"Thanks for coming to my parade!" she winked at the cheering crowd. "High-fives for everyone!"

Supergirl glided low over the crowd, slapping the open palms of her fans. The rapid slaps sounded like popping corn.

"Wonder what it feels like to be admired by so many," Lois quietly sighed. "What do you think, Clark? Uh, now where'd he go?"

Clark Kent was already moving faster than the human eye. He quickly changed from his business suit to reveal his Superman outfit beneath.

Among all the excitement, no one else had noticed the tall man in the raincoat and hat walking through the crowd toward Supergirl. Superman flew toward the criminal, but not before the man's fingers made contact with the hand of Supergirl.

"Parasite!"

Supergirl groaned and immediately grew weaker. She tumbled helplessly across the sidewalk, merely from a single sinister touch of the stranger's hand. Parasite had absorbed Supergirl's powers. His purple skin glowed brighter. His muscles grew larger. With a shout of triumph, he turned to face the Man of Steel.

"Don't you dare harm her!" Superman shouted as he landed next to the villain.

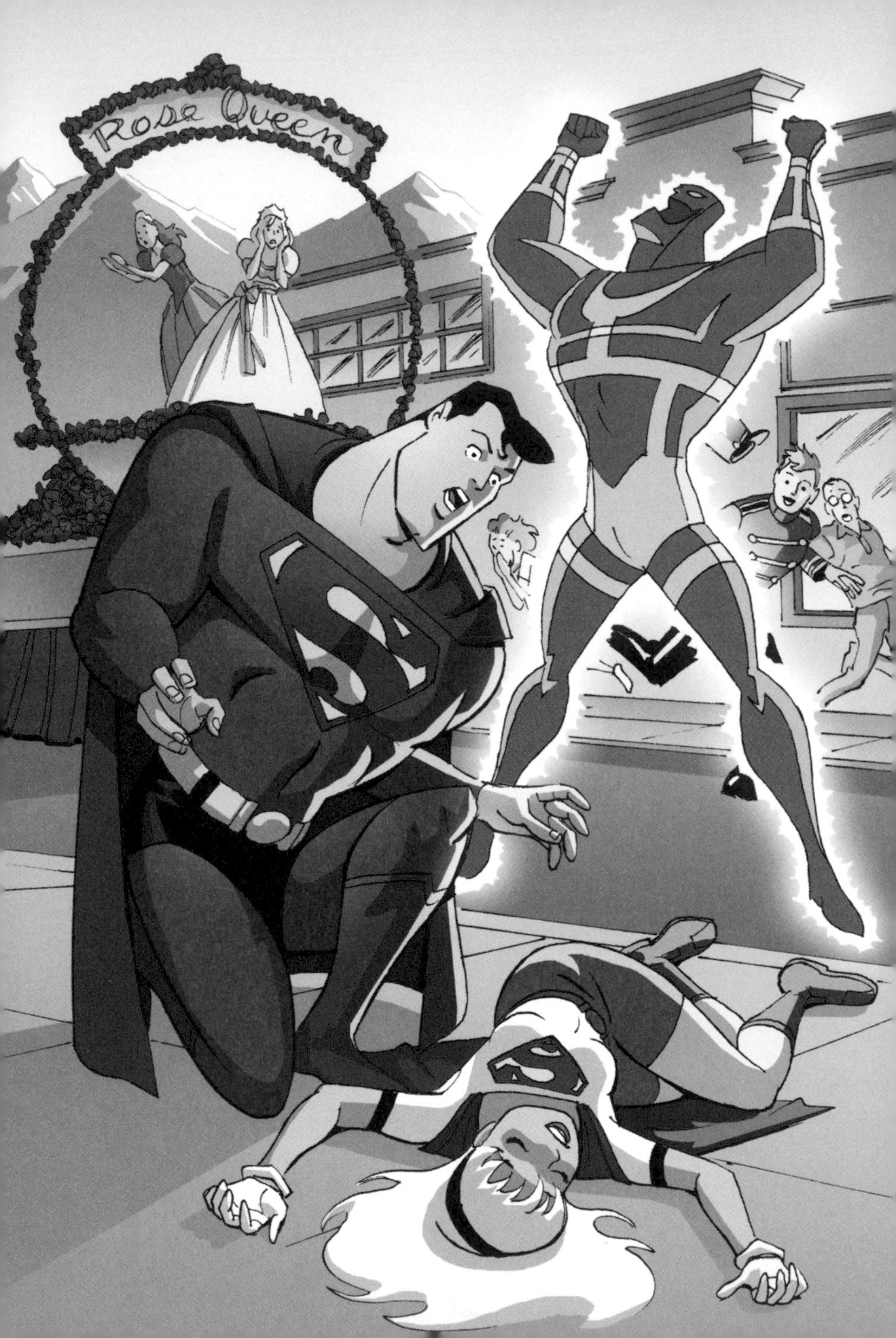
Rose Queen

Superman barely saw the punch coming. Parasite's fist was as fast and explosive as a lightning bolt. The Man of Steel crashed down with the sound of an avalanche. Parasite threw away his coat and hat. His terrible eyes glared with hatred.

"Don't know about the rest of you," Parasite said with a laugh, "but I feel just super!"

CHAPTER 5

THE WAR THAT SHOOK EARTH

"Don't bother getting up, Superman," Parasite growled. "I already have Supergirl's strength. You can't win."

Superman shook the concrete dust from his hair, clearing his aching head. Parasite walked toward him. His muscles moved like pythons under his purple skin. Supergirl lay limp on the pavement, drained of her powers.

The crowd had run away. *Good,* Superman thought. *One less thing to worry about.*

With each powerful step, Parasite created a small crater in the sidewalk. His laughter rumbled like thunder.

Superman got to his feet. He had to stay away from the monster's hands, or his own strength would be drained. How could he fight an enemy that he dared not touch? This wasn't going to be easy.

Superman stared at Parasite. The hero's eyes became twin suns, as his heat vision melted the asphalt in the street into glowing lava. *HISSSSSS*

Superman scooped up the bubbling asphalt. He quickly wrapped it around Parasite like a flaming cocoon. Using his super-breath, Superman cooled the asphalt in an instant. The cocoon was now as hard as rock.

Superman knew he had to move this fight far away, to protect the townspeople of Swan Valley. Supergirl still wasn't moving. She was stretched out on the sidewalk, barely breathing. How could he leave her?

Parasite was beginning to struggle inside his asphalt prison. Superman uprooted a telephone pole and swung it as easily as a baseball bat. With a mighty blow, he sent Parasite into orbit.

Now Superman had a few precious seconds to tend to Supergirl. As he flew to his cousin, a surprise greeted him. Lois Lane had arrived there first.

"Don't worry," Lois said. She gently held Supergirl's head. "I'll take care of her."

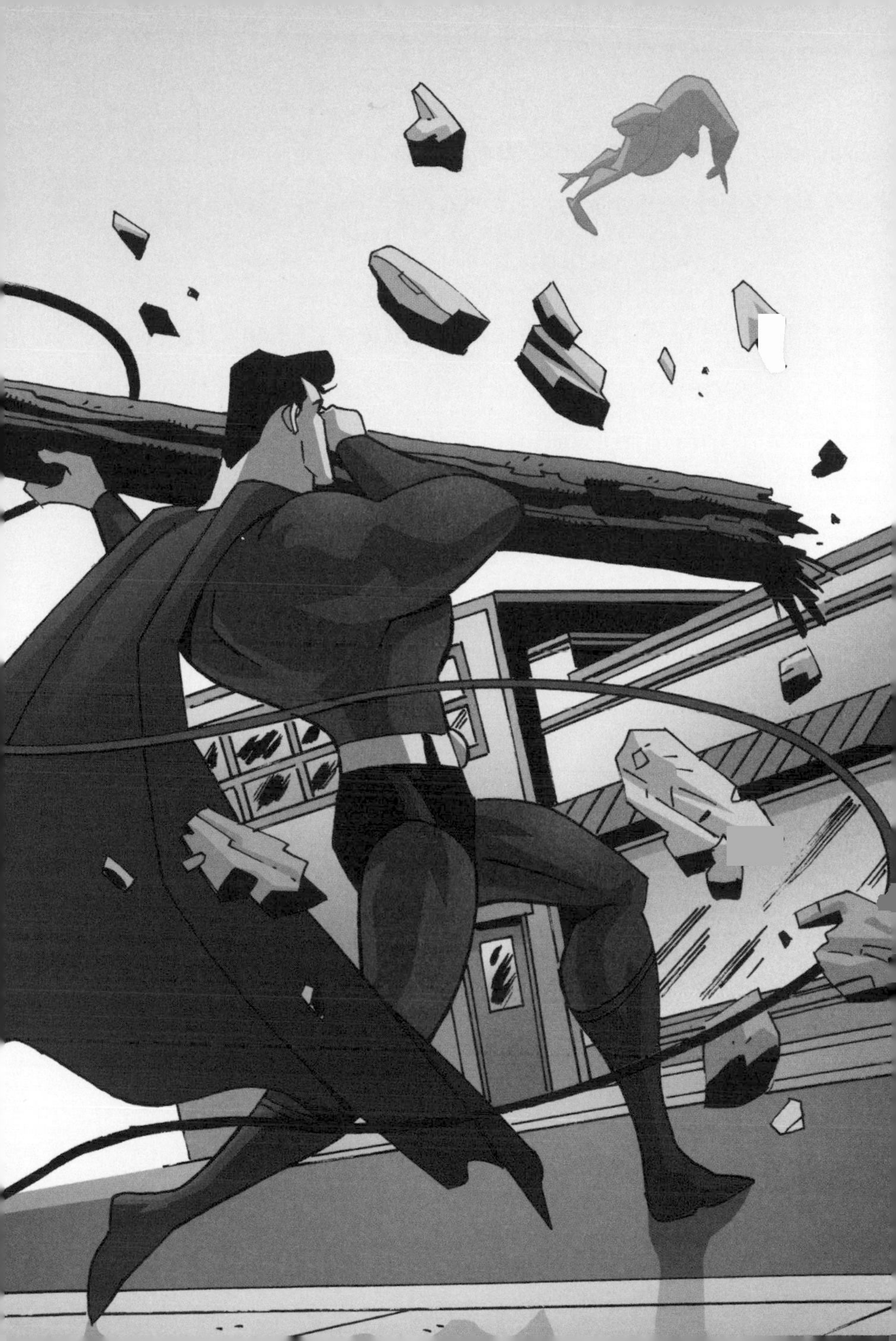

"That monster has to be stopped," Lois said to Superman. "And you're the only one who can do it!"

The Man of Steel nodded at Lois. He was gone in a flash, hunting Parasite in the upper atmosphere. From below, Lois could hear explosions high above the clouds. It was the sound of a mighty battle.

"What would we ever do without him?" Lois said softly to herself. "What would any of us do?"

• • •

Far away, near the North Pole, Superman crashed to Earth and collided with a glacier. Huge chunks of ice flew through the air. Clouds of snow billowed into the sky. Superman's fall had created a huge valley in the center of the glacier. Parasite followed closely behind the hero.

With heat-beams from his eyes, the purple villain turned the icy valley into a boiling cauldron. Walls of snow and ice turned instantly into water and crashed down onto the Man of Steel. The freezing water stung his skin. The mighty flood hit him with the force of an iron wall. With a powerful surge, he shot through the churning water and rocketed into the sky.

Parasite's newly acquired powers would last for only a couple hours, rapidly burning away like calories. Superman had to keep him fighting until the effect of Supergirl's strength wore off, but time wasn't on his side. How much longer could he avoid touching Parasite?

Superman hurled an iceberg at his enemy.

The tremendous impact had no effect. Parasite was much too strong. Superman felt as if he were fighting himself.

Suddenly Superman felt the grip of the Parasite's hands upon his throat. The villain's fingers felt like steel. Like his own!

"You couldn't stay away from me forever, Superman!" Parasite said. "It was only a matter of time before I got my hands on you. Now all your powers will be mine!"

Sorely exhausted, the Man of Steel heroically struggled against the monster, but already he felt his strength draining away. The yellow sun, which gave him his superpowers, was low in the sky. Its rays were too weak to help him. The sound of Parasite's laughter seemed to fade into the darkness falling before his eyes. He couldn't give up. There must be a way to win.

A blonde-haired teenager had the answer. "Looks like you could use a hand, Parasite!" said Supergirl. She flew within his reach, letting the monster grab hold of her. "Lucky for me, you guys left an easy trail to follow!"

Parasite held them both in a deadly grasp. Power flowed into him unlike anything he'd ever imagined. Pure volcanic, continent-lifting strength burst through his muscles. The sound of his own bloodstream trumpeted uncontrollably in his super-sensitive eardrums. Parasite's eyes grew wide, suddenly seeing across a thousand galaxies, dazzled by a million suns. It was too much power.

Parasite screamed, releasing them.

"Superman!" he cried. "Help me!"

A sudden burst of light filled the air. The combined powers of Superman and Supergirl caused Parasite to short-circuit. He slumped to the ground, unconscious and groaning softly. Superman and Supergirl stood above him on the icy landscape.

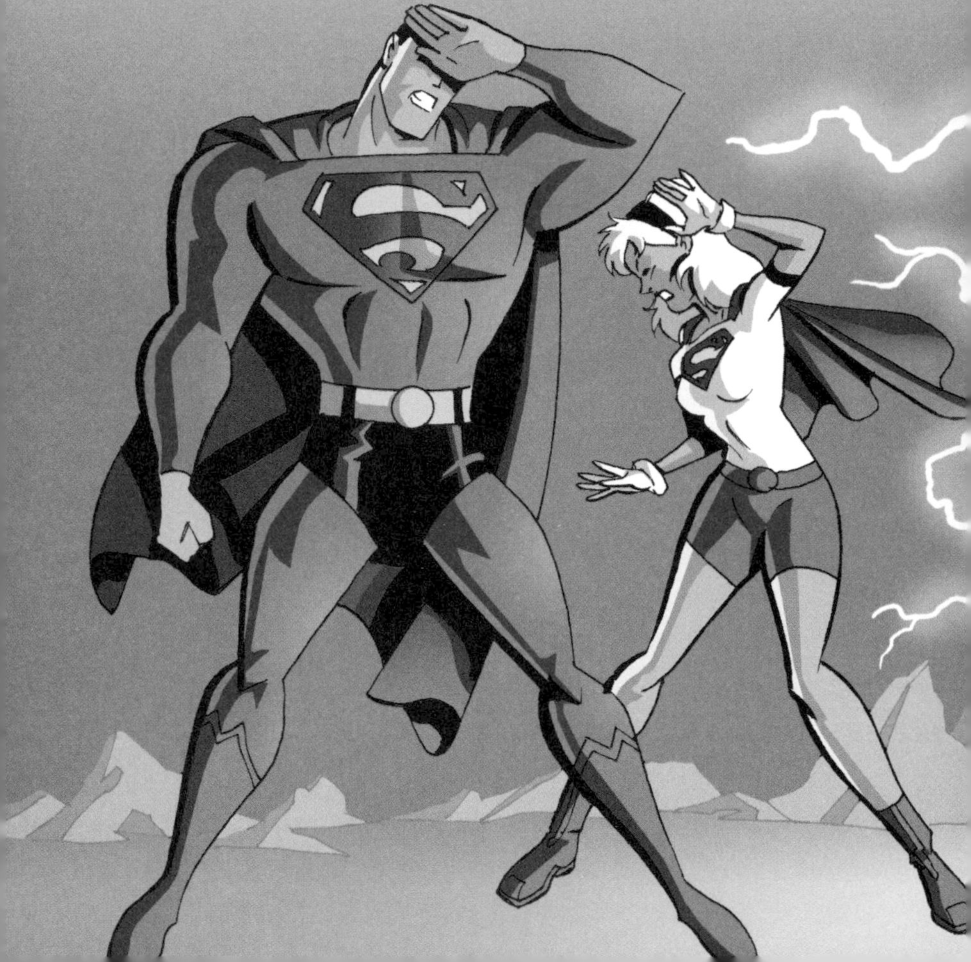

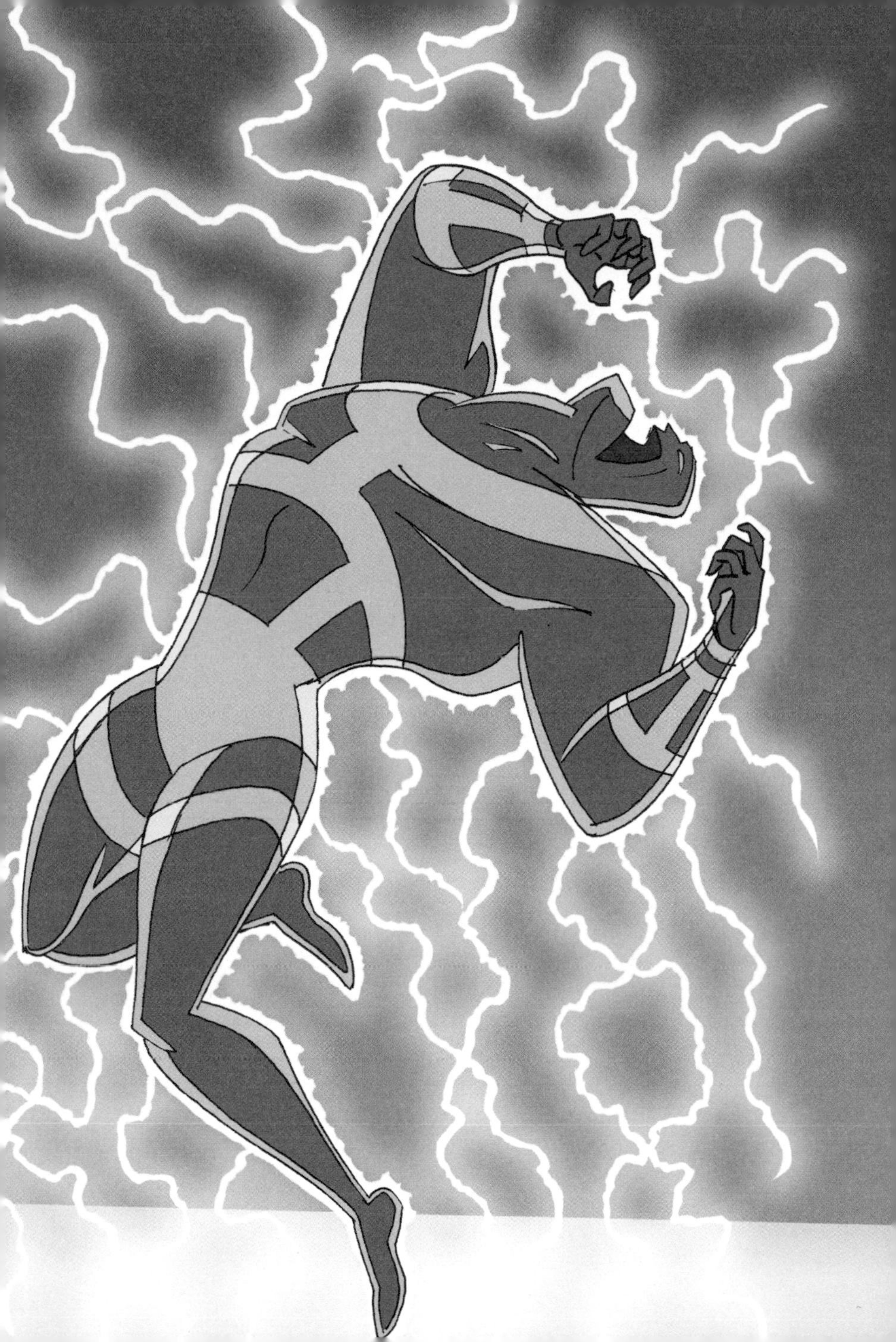

Shortly after, Superman arrived at the Fortress of Solitude, his secret refuge in the Arctic. It was the only place where he could find a few precious moments of quiet and peace. At times, the fortress had seemed too quiet, too lonely. Now the secret halls had a welcome visitor.

"This place is amazing," said Supergirl.

"You're the only other person who's seen it," said Superman.

"Really?" she asked.

The Man of Steel nodded. "You're family," he said.

"And that's the only way we could have defeated that monster," Supergirl pointed out. "Because we are family. I figured there was no way the Parasite could absorb both of our superpowers at the same time."

"The cousins from Krypton were just too much for him." She smiled and added, "When he goes back to prison, I just hope they put a better lock on his cell next time."

The teenager had been talking nonstop for almost an hour. She looked around at the giant rooms filled with scientific equipment and souvenirs from other planets.

"I'll bet your friend Lois Lane would love to get her eyes on this place," she said. "It would make a terrific news story."

Superman wasn't listening. Instead, he looked as if he could hear something from very far away.

Suddenly, he took flight.

"Hey! Where're you going?" Supergirl yelled.

"An ocean liner is under attack in the Pacific," he said. "It's modern-day pirates. They're using rocket and laser rifles. I could probably use some help. Of course, if you have other plans —"

Supergirl leaped into the air, racing after him.

"Are you kidding?" she laughed. "What's family for?"

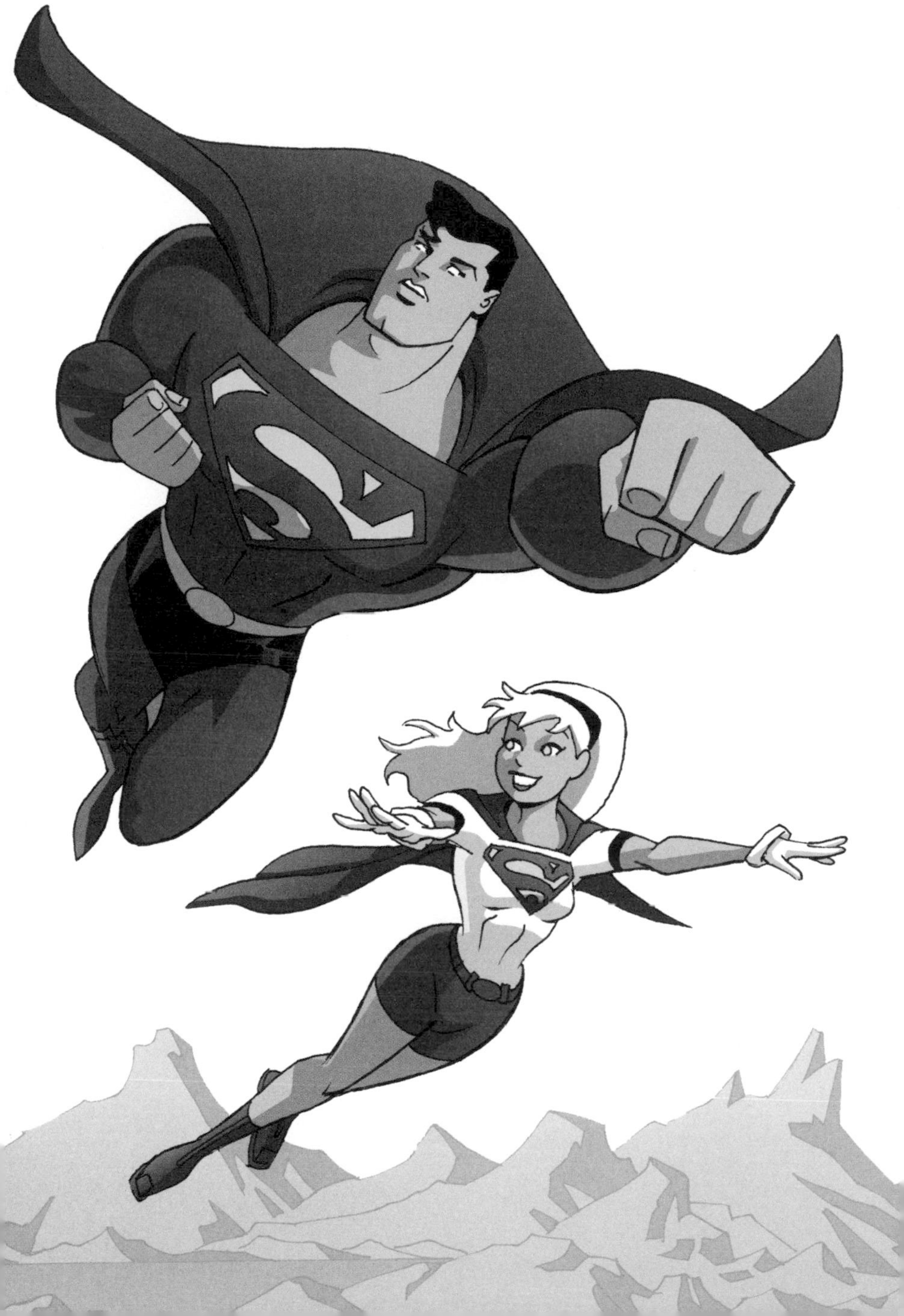

DAILY PLANET

FROM THE DESK OF CLARK KENT

WHO IS PARASITE?

As Rudy Jones's gambling addiction grew, so did his debts. To pay them off, he attempted to steal experimental chemicals from a laboratory in Metropolis. When Superman intervened, Rudy fled. During his escape, he accidentally exposed himself to toxic liquids, transforming him into the power-hungry monster Parasite. Forever altered, Rudy developed a new addiction: the desire for power. Parasite must regularly feed on the energy of others, or he will wither and die.

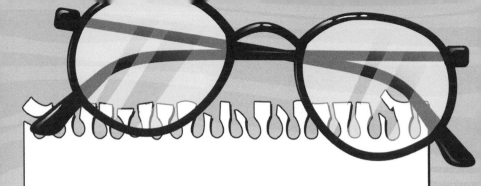

- Parasite poses a unique problem to anyone who stands in his way: his energy-sucking, parasitic powers let him rise to the level of any foe simply by touching them. The more powerful his opponent is, the more threatening Parasite becomes.

- Parasite possesses the ability to steal the thoughts of his victims in addition to their powers. If Parasite ever drained enough of Superman's strength, he would discover the Man of Steel's true identity!

- Having grown bored with siphoning human energy, Parasite went after Mr. Mxyzptlk, the mischievous, magical imp from the Fifth Dimension. Upon stealing Mxy's strange powers, he spread chaos across Metropolis, turning Lois Lane and Jimmy Olsen into super-villains. He even made a Superman statue come to life!

- Once Parasite tasted Superman's massive power, he knew no other energy would ever satisfy him. Parasite will do whatever it takes to once again get within reach of the Man of Steel, or his super-powered cousin, Supergirl.

BIOGRAPHIES

Martin Powell has been a freelance writer since 1986. He has written hundreds of stories, many of which have been published by Disney, Marvel, Tekno Comics, Moonstone Books, and others. In 1989, Powell received an Eisner Award nomination for his graphic novel *Scarlet in Gaslight*. This award is one of the highest comic book honors.

Rick Burchett has worked as a comics artist for over 25 years. He has received the comics industry's Eisner Award three times, Spain's Haxtur Award, and he has been nominated for England's Eagle award. Rick lives with his wife and two sons near St. Louis, Missouri.

Lee Loughridge has been working in comics for over 14 years. He currently lives in sunny California in a tent on the beach.

GLOSSARY

cauldron (KAWL-druhn)—a large cooking pot

cocoon (kuh-KOON)—a covering that surrounds something entirely

dynamo (DYE-nuh-moh)—an energetic, forceful person who works very hard

foundation (foun-DAY-shuhn)—a solid structure on which something is built

parasite (PA-ruh-site)—something that steals its food or energy by feeding on a host, or victim

sinister (SIN-uh-stur)—evil or threatening

sonic boom (SON-ik BOOM)—the loud noise produced by something when it travels faster than the speed of sound

tinderbox (TIN-der-boks)—a small box that is used for starting fires

triumph (TRYE-uhmf)—a great victory, success, or achievement

villain (VIL-uhn)—a wicked or evil person

DISCUSSION QUESTIONS

1. Supergirl often learns lessons from her older cousin Superman. What lessons did she learn in this story?

2. In this book, Supergirl helps Superman defeat Parasite. Do you think the Man of Steel could have defeated the villain alone? Why or why not?

3. Clark Kent is secretly Superman. Why do you think he keeps his identity a secret? If you were a super hero, would you tell anyone?

WRITING PROMPTS

1. Supergirl is the cousin of Superman. Write a story about one of your own family members. How have they helped you?

2. Write your own story about Supergirl. Who will she help Superman defeat next time? You decide.

3. Besides having superpowers, Supergirl is just an average kid. If you were a super hero, what superpowers would you have? What would your super hero name be?

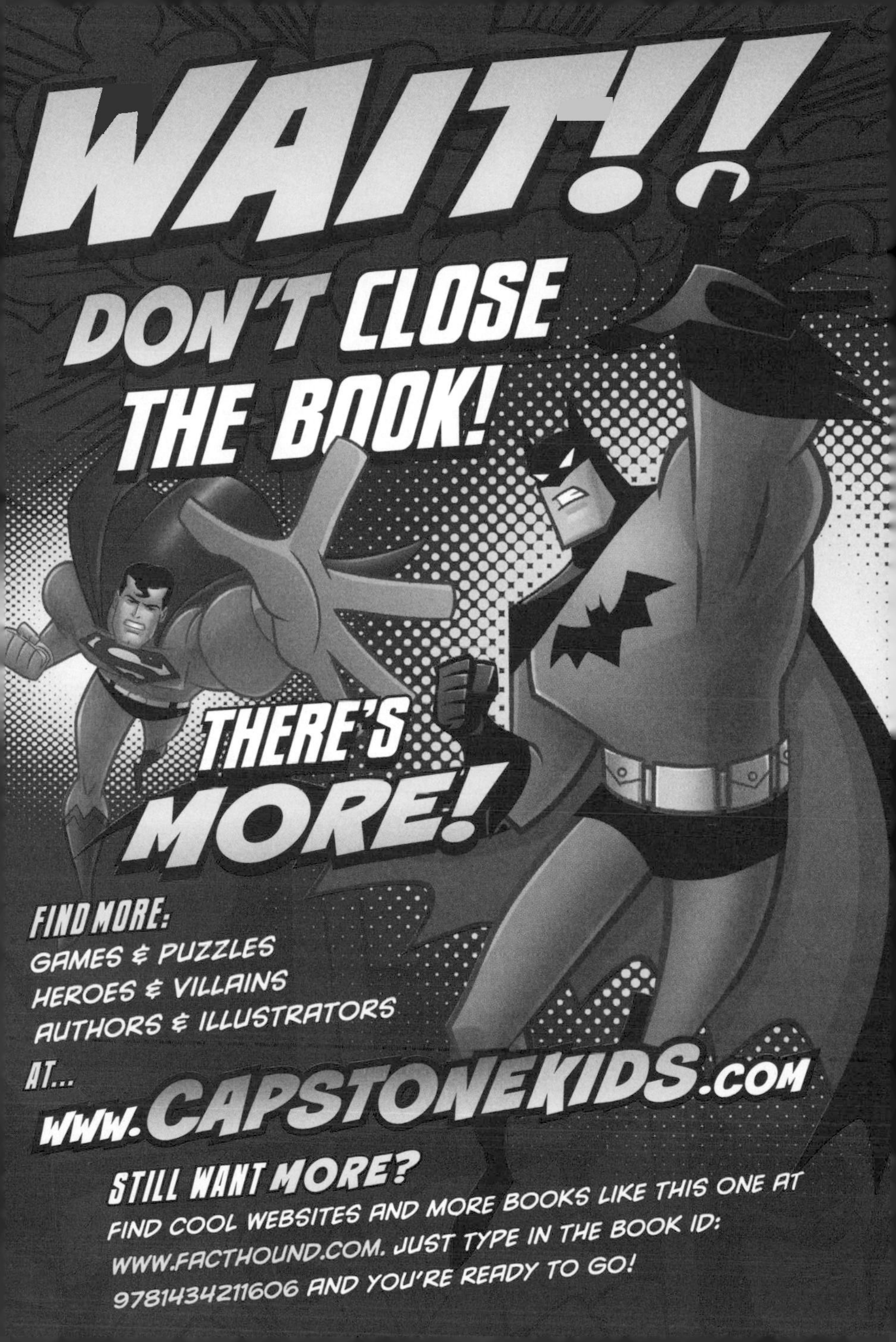
WAIT!!
DON'T CLOSE THE BOOK!
THERE'S MORE!
FIND MORE:
GAMES & PUZZLES
HEROES & VILLAINS
AUTHORS & ILLUSTRATORS
AT...
WWW.CAPSTONEKIDS.COM
STILL WANT MORE?
FIND COOL WEBSITES AND MORE BOOKS LIKE THIS ONE AT
WWW.FACTHOUND.COM. JUST TYPE IN THE BOOK ID:
9781434211606 AND YOU'RE READY TO GO!

MORE NEW SUPERMAN ADVENTURES!

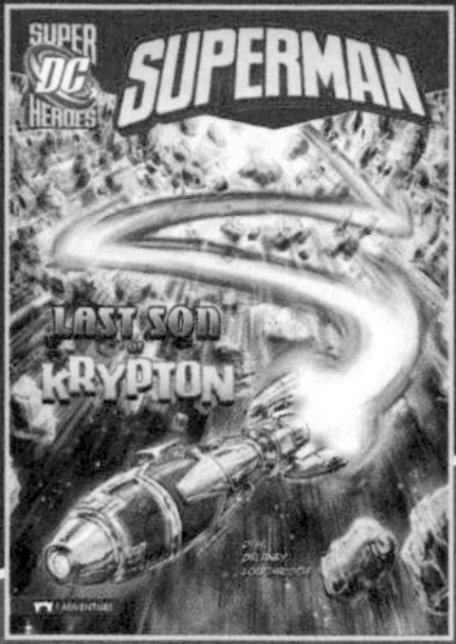
SUPER DC HEROES
SUPERMAN
LAST SON KRYPTON
LAST SON OF KRYPTON

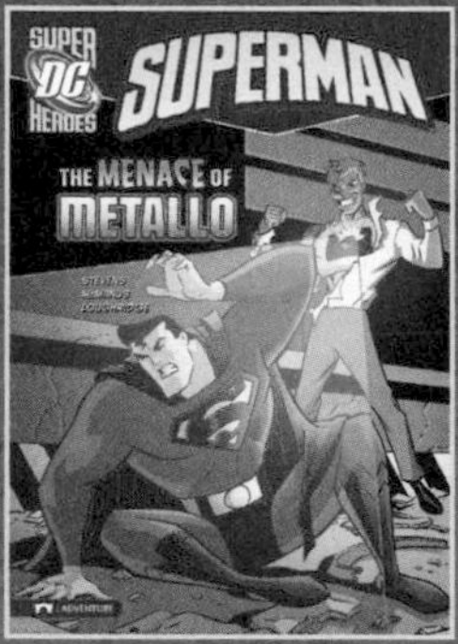
SUPER DC HEROES
SUPERMAN
THE MENACE OF METALLO
THE MENACE OF METALLO

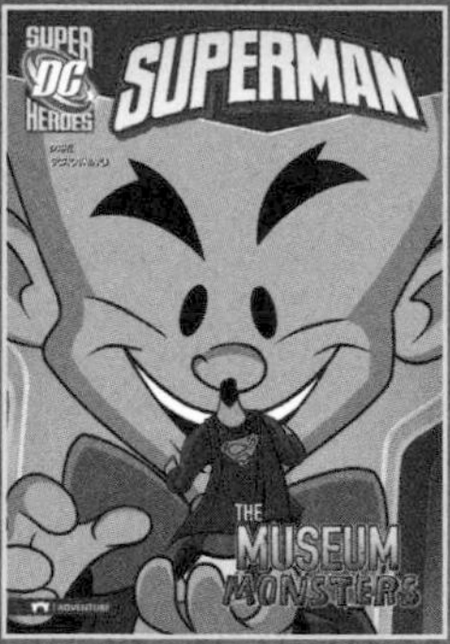
SUPER DC HEROES
SUPERMAN
THE MUSEUM MONSTERS
THE MUSEUM MONSTERS

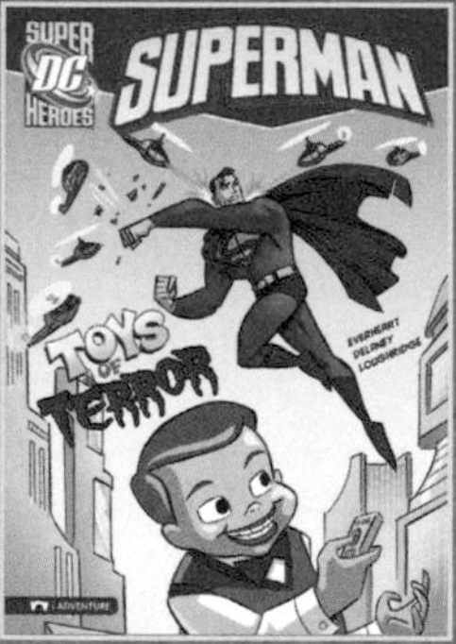
SUPER DC HEROES
SUPERMAN
TOYS OF TERROR
TOYS OF TERROR

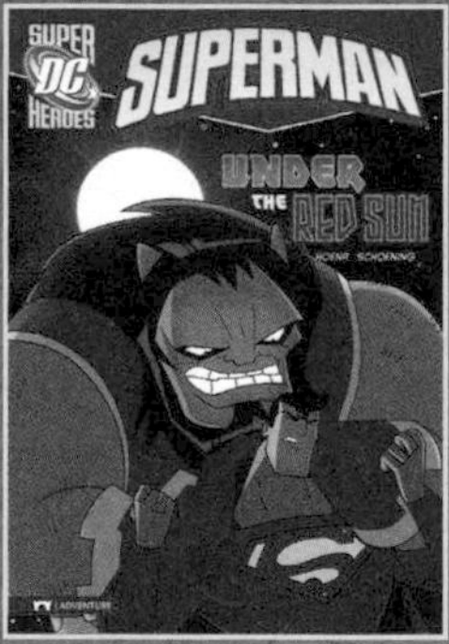
SUPER DC HEROES
SUPERMAN
UNDER THE RED SUN
UNDER THE RED SUN

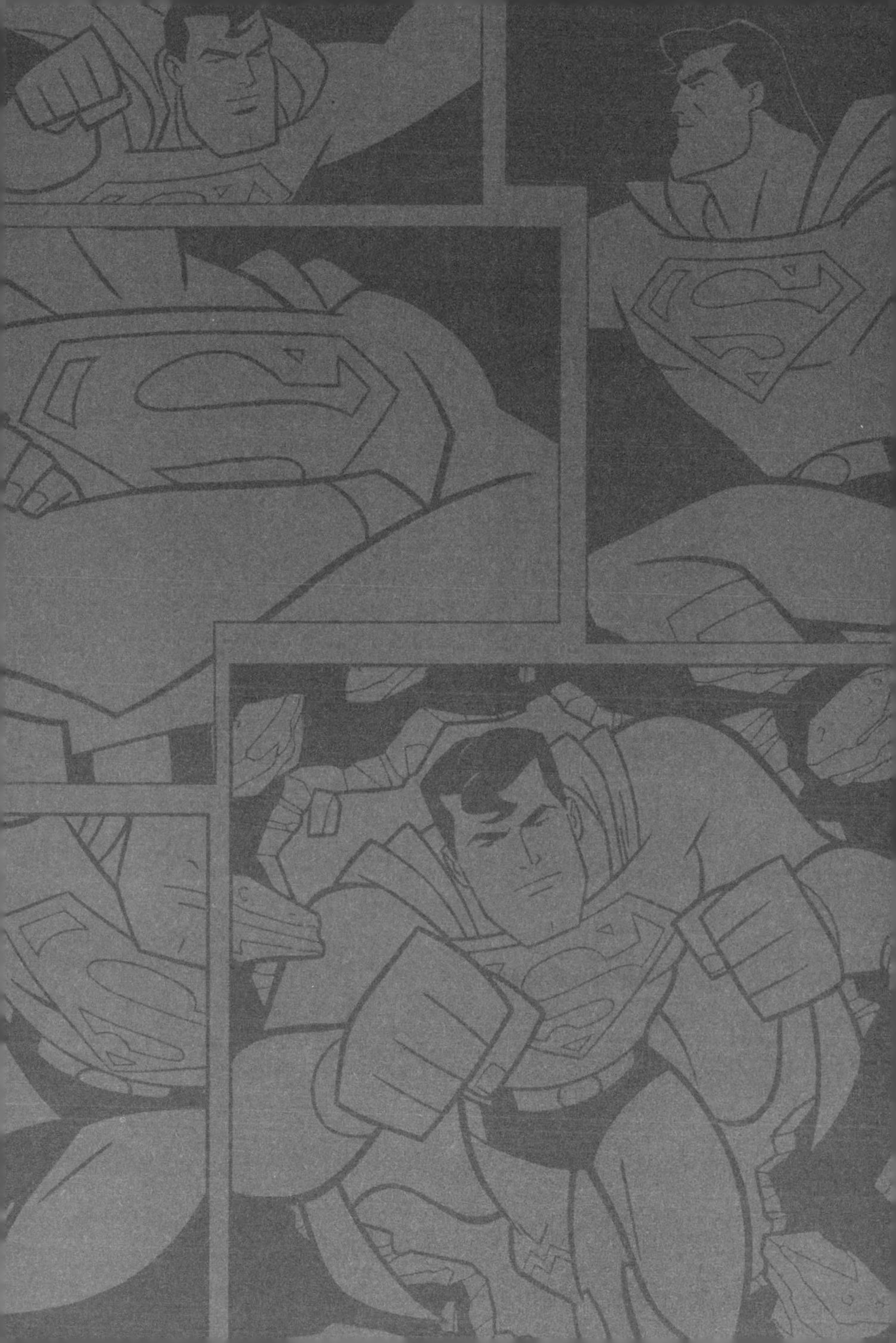

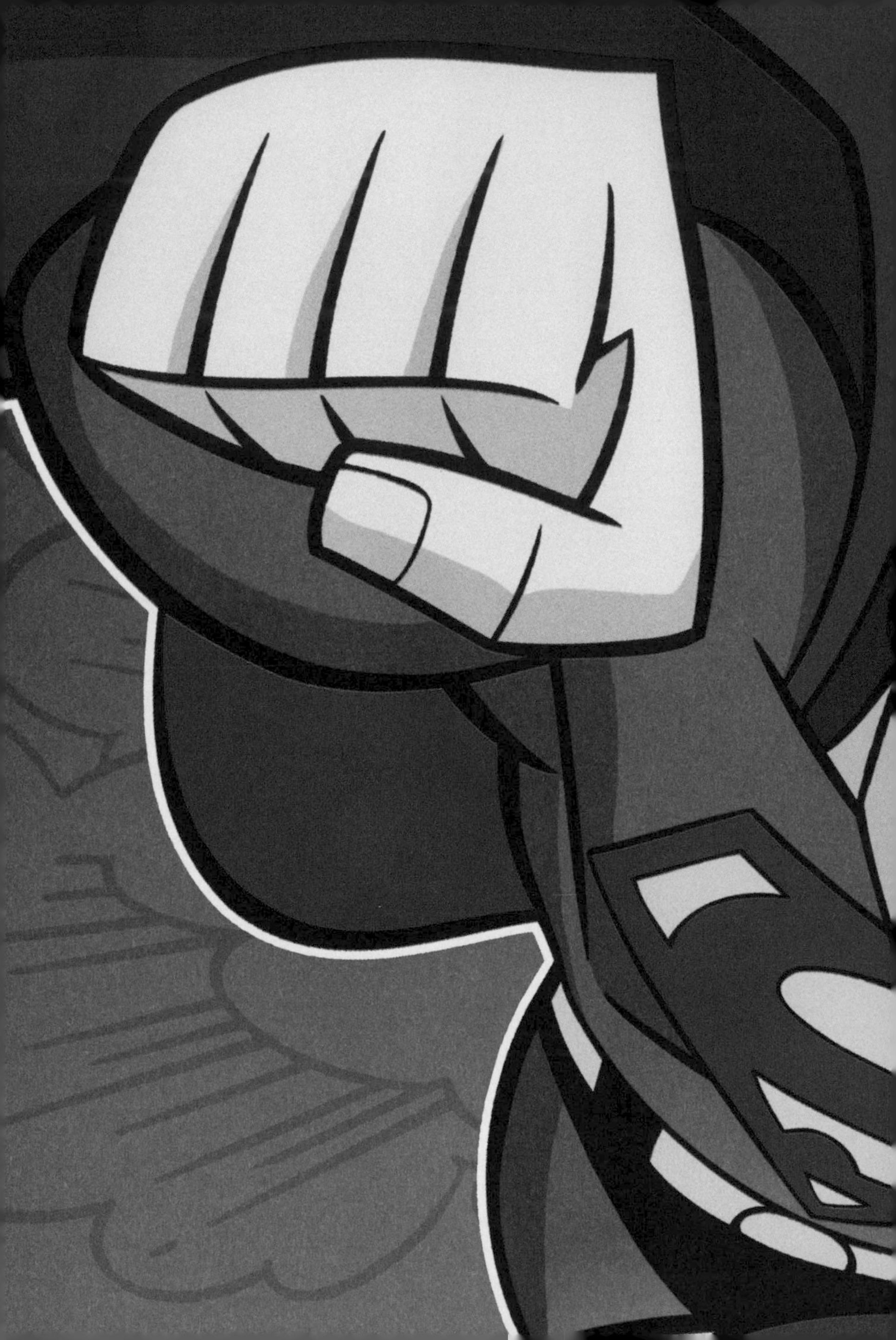

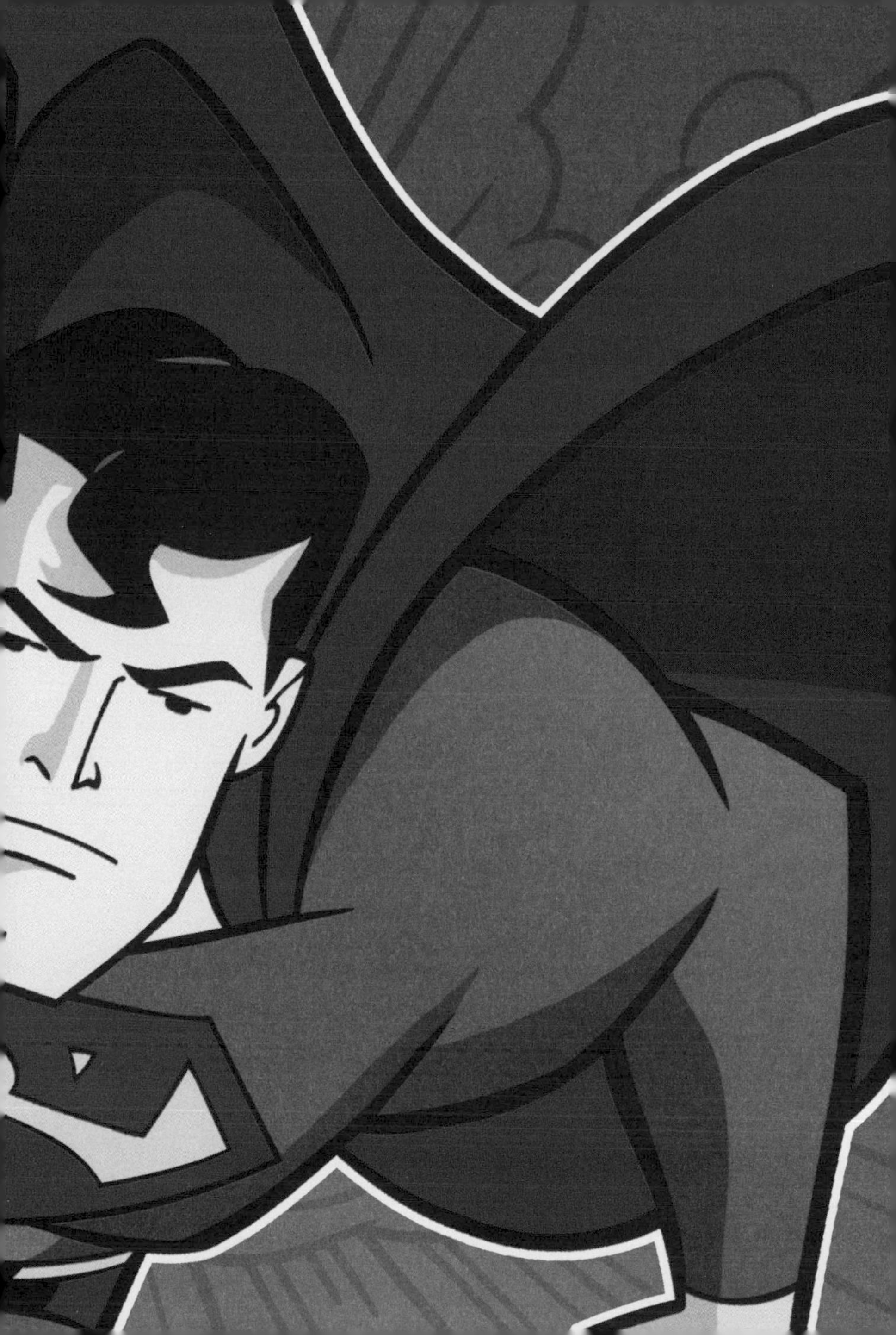